CINDY

BRADLEY

BIFF

Early Monday morning, at school . . .

GO OSTRICHES!!

●ASSEMBLY TODAY: YOUR DISMAL FUTURE

ATTENDANCE MANDATORY!

RUSTLE, SCHT IKK!

What are you doing, Dwight?

RRAAAWWR!

Not funny.

Then . . .

SQWEEEEE

Is this thing on?

All right, students, listen up.

I've got good news and bad news.

Mostly bad.

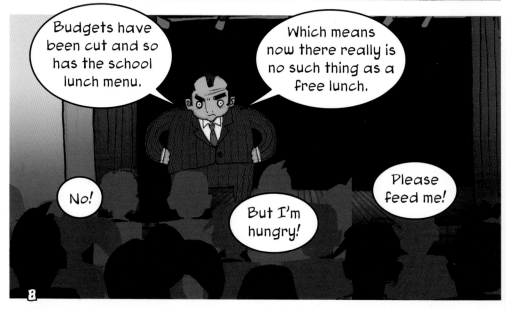

Budgets have been cut and so has the school lunch menu.

Which means now there really is no such thing as a free lunch.

No!

But I'm hungry!

Please feed me!

9

19

Soon . . .

Oh, all right, give me two of the Crumple bars.

Later, at school . . .

A THOUSAND POUNDS?!

How do you sell a thousand pounds worth of candy?

Obviously, **you** don't. But Bradley is gifted.

I'm going to tell the lunch lady she can go ahead and place that order for liver nuggets.

This isn't right. Bradley's cheating somehow.

I say today after school, we follow him.

24

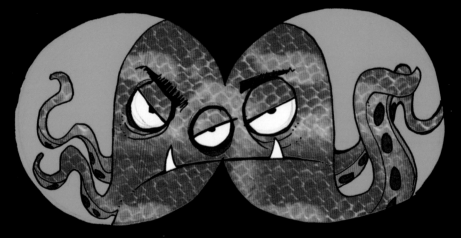

Twenty minutes later, at school . . .

CANDY FOR SALE

clip, tick,

NDY FOR SALE

clip, clip, c

THUMP!
THUM

Where do you think you're going?

29

HOW TO DRAW A MONSTER

YOU'LL NEED:

- a pencil
- a piece of paper
- a rubber (or two!)

1.

Some monsters look like giant blobs of slime! For this monster, start by drawing a large jellybean shape on the piece of paper.

2.

Next, connect some squiggly lines to the base of the jellybean shape. These will be the monster's tentacles. An octopus has eight tentacles, but your monster can have any number.

3.

After the tentacles are attached, give your monster some eyeballs and a mouth. Add sharp fangs to make your monster really mean.

4. Next, draw details on your creepy creature. Maybe add a few scales or some suckers on the tentacles.

5. When your monster is almost finished, colour in its slimy skin. A pink monster could be pretty or a green monster could be gross. You decide!

6. Your monster is finished! Now, give him a name. This one's called Biff.

AUTHOR

Robert Marsh grew up in Omaha, Nebraska, USA, but longed to live somewhere else. He pretended not to live in Omaha by reading lots of books. Every week, Marsh checked out 20 books from the library. As he didn't have time to read all of those books, he would read the first chapter of each and make up the rest of the story. Marsh now makes up stories for a living and doesn't live in Omaha. Dreams do come true.

ILLUSTRATOR

Tom Percival grew up in Shropshire, a place of such remarkable beauty that he decided to sit in his room every day, drawing pictures and writing stories. But that was a long time ago, and much has changed since then. Now, Percival lives in Bristol, where he sits in his room all day, drawing pictures and writing stories. His patient girlfriend, Liz, and their baby son, Ethan, keep him company.

GLOSSARY

allergic if you are allergic to something, it causes you to have an unpleasant reaction of some kind

competition a contest of some kind

evidence information or facts that help you prove something or make you believe that something is true

gifted if you are gifted, you have a special talent

recon short for reconaissance, which means gathering information in secret

scam a scheme or trick used to make a quick profit

shakedown the act of taking money from a person by force

suspect someone thought to be responsible for a crime

DISCUSSION QUESTIONS

1. Dwight is allergic to chocolate. Do you know anyone who has an allergy? What are they allergic to?

2. Does your school hold fundraisers? What would you want to sell to raise money?

3. Each page of this book has several illustrations called panels. Which panel is your favourite? Why?

WRITING PROMPTS

1. Gabby and Dwight end up eating candy and chocolate for school lunches! If you could make your school's lunch menu, what would you serve your fellow students each day? Write a menu that lists a meal for each day of the school week.

2. Gabby catches Bradley trying to cheat his way to victory in the school fundraiser competition. Have you ever cheated at anything? Have you ever caught someone else? Write about your experience.

3. There's a new monster in town — yours! Draw a picture of your new friend. What does it eat? What does it like to do in its spare time? Write a brief story about your monster.